To our three grown-up monsters:
Zachary, Jesse, and Rayanne
—D.V.

For my two little non-monsters and for my wife
for putting up with a snoring monster
—Z.O.

THIS IS A BORZOI BOOK PUBLISHED BY ALFRED A. KNOPF

Text copyright © 2017 by Denise Vega
Jacket art and interior illustrations copyright © 2017 by Zachariah OHora

Visit us on the Web! randomhousekids.com
Educators and librarians, for a variety of teaching tools, visit us at RHTeachersLibrarians.com

Library of Congress Cataloging-in-Publication Data
Names: Vega, Denise, author. | OHora, Zachariah, illustrator.
Title: If your monster won't go to bed / Denise Vega, Zachariah OHora.
Other titles: If your monster will not go to bed
Description: First edition. | New York : Alfred A. Knopf, [2017] | "2015" |
Summary: A handbook for youngsters that includes such instructions as "pour your monster a nice
big glass of calming, crunchy, oozy bug juice slimed with ooey-gooey snail trails."
Identifiers: LCCN 2015024303 | ISBN 978-0-553-49655-0 (trade) | ISBN 978-0-553-49656-7 (lib. bdg.)
| ISBN 978-0-553-49657-4 (ebook)
Subjects: | CYAC: Bedtime—Fiction. | Monsters—Fiction. | Humorous stories.
Classification: LCC PZ7.V4865 If 2017 | DDC [E]—dc23

The illustrations in this book were created using acrylic paint on 140-lb. BFK Rives printing paper.
You read that right, just old-school paint on paper.

MANUFACTURED IN CHINA
March 2017
10 9 8 7 6 5 4 3 2 1   First Edition

IF YOUR MONSTER WON'T GO TO BED

WRITTEN BY
DENISE VEGA

ILLUSTRATED BY
ZACHARIAH OHORA

Alfred A. Knopf 🐕 New York

TIME FOR BED!

Who hates those words more than anything?
That's right. Your monster.
But we all know what happens when a monster doesn't get enough sleep: massive monster tantrums, refusing to join the Sneak-Up-and-Scare-Your-Sister game, and falling asleep in his slug mush.

Let's review a bedtime routine guaranteed to help any monster drift off into peaceful nightmare-land, rested and ready to play toss-the-slime-ball with the rest of the kids and monsters.

Don't ask your parents to help you. They know a lot about putting kids to bed, but nothing about putting *monsters* to bed. It's not their fault; they're just not good at it.

Don't bring in your dog to cuddle. She'll bark and whine and chase your monster's tail, and your monster will growl and snarl and chase your dog's tail, which will lead to a monster meltdown. And who wants that (besides other monsters)?

YIP! YIP!

Don't do the Monster Stomp.

Your monster will wiggle his waggle, flick his fur, and clench his claws, and the next thing you know he'll be shaking his bristly bottom and won't want to stop.

And you'll be shaking your *un*-bristly bottom, so it will be a big bottom-shaking, waggle-wiggling, fur-flicking, claw-clenching Monster-Kid Stomp, which will last all night. Save the Monster Stomp for daytime fun.

Don't have your monster count sheep.
You know what will happen. And sheep
aren't good for a monster's digestion.
All that wool makes him gassy.

Don't give your monster a glass of milk. Monsters hate milk unless it's sour and green and smells like dirty underwear.

And if you give them sour, green, dirty-underwear-smelling milk, they'll stay up all night burping sour, green, dirty-underwear-smelling burps—and who wants that (besides other you-know-whats)?

I know that's lots
of DON'Ts. So if your
monster won't go to
bed, what do you DO?

Step 1

Pour your monster a nice big glass of calming, crunchy, oozy bug juice slimed with ooey-gooey snail trails. No monster can resist this. (And maybe you can't either? Go ahead. Take a sip.)

WHIRR!

Step 2

Give your monster an ice-cold, shiver-inducing bath to relax him—and make sure to scrub behind his ears with mud soap.

Step 3

Brush your monster's fangs until they are at their smelly, rotten best. And don't forget to floss!

Step 4

Help your monster find his favorite squishy, squashy, can't-go-to-bed-without-it toy. Put all the other monster toys in your parents' bed. They will appreciate your thoughtfulness.

Step 5

Read the freakiest, creepiest, scariest story from your bookshelf—screaming where appropriate—and watch your monster's eyelids droop. If your monster asks for one more story, shout "*NO WAY!*" and get ready for . . .

Step 6

In the key of screech,

sing "Shock-a-Bye, Monster"

and listen to those gigantic

monster snores (along

with the snores of your

family and maybe even

the whole block!).

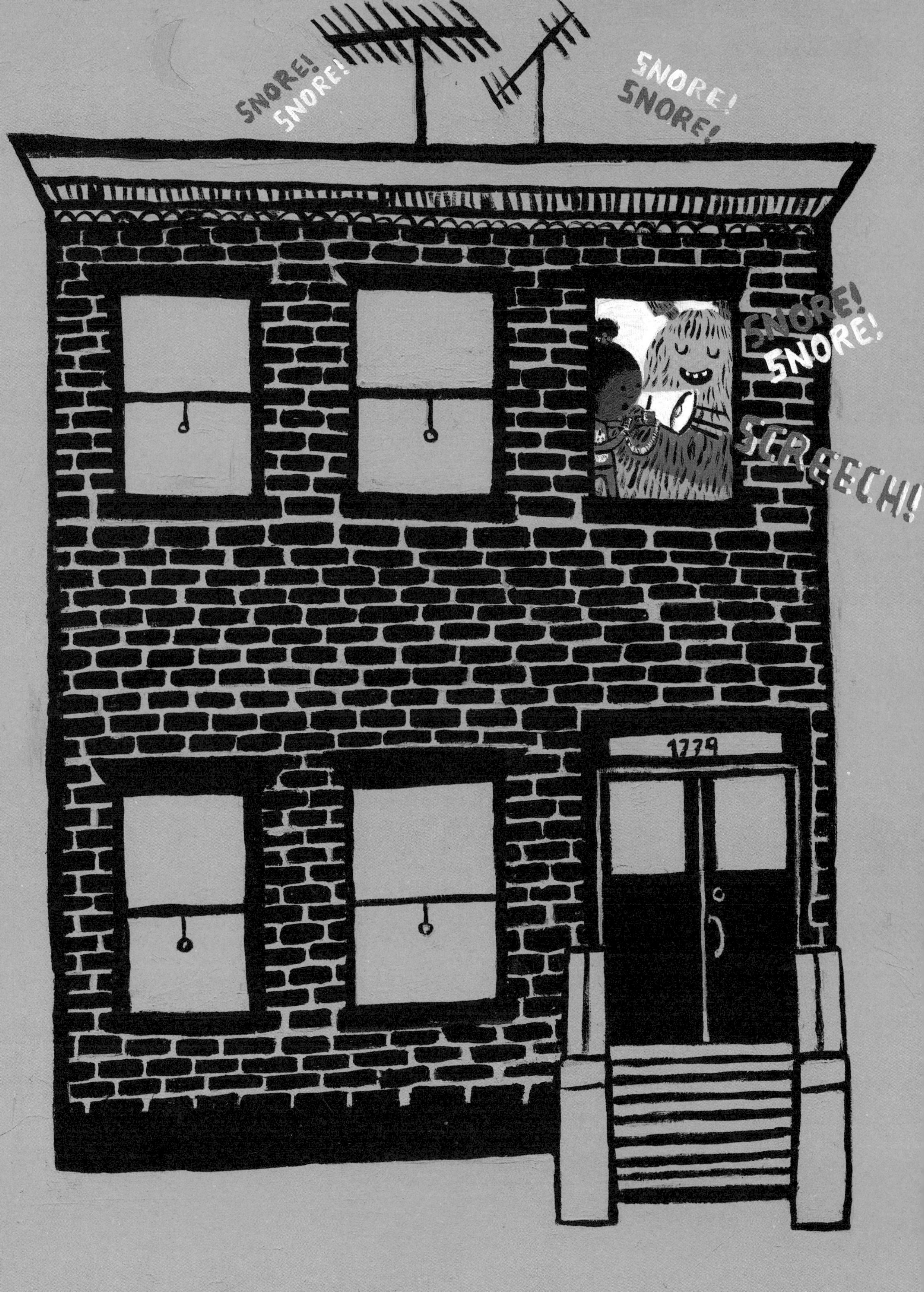
SNORE!
SNORE!
SNORE!
SNORE!
SNORE!
SNORE!
SCREECH!
1779

Congratulations, you've done it! Your monster has officially gone to bed.

You are the Master of Monsters, the Captain of Creatures, the Baron(ess) of Boogie Men! You're so good, everyone in your neighborhood will start asking you to help with *their* monsters.

Uh-oh.

Looks like that dragon won't put on her pajamas.

And that werewolf won't stop howling.

And that zombie is annoying the whole family.

I know a lot about monsters, but nothing about dragons or werewolves or zombies.

I'm outta here.